EXIT
EXIT
FOR SALE
KEEP OUT!
PRIVATE PROPERTY
ADMIT ONE
ORANGE
JUICE
MEOW MEOW
S
P
SLOW
HOME
VISITOR
REPORT CARD

David Mortimore Baxter

by Karen Tayleur

illustrated by Brann Garvey

Spies

Librarian Reviewer
Laurie K. Holland
Media Specialist (National Board Certified), Edina, MN
MA in Elementary Education, Minnesota State University, Mankato

Reading Consultant
Elizabeth Stedem
Educator/Consultant, Colorado Springs, CO
MA in Elementary Education, University of Denver, CO

STONE ARCH BOOKS
Minneapolis San Diego

David Mortimore Baxter is published by Stone Arch Books
151 Good Counsel Drive, P.O. Box 669
Mankato, Minnesota 56002
www.stonearchbooks.com

Library of Congress Cataloging-in-Publication Data
Tayleur, Karen.
Spies!: David Mortimore Baxter Cracks the Case / by Karen Tayleur; illustrated by Brann Garvey.
p. cm. -- (David Mortimore Baxter)
ISBN 978-1-4342-0462-2 (library binding)
ISBN 978-1-4342-0512-4 (paperback)
[1. Mystery and detective stories. 2. Humorous stories.] I. Garvey, Brann, ill. II. Title.
PZ7.T21149Spi 2008
[Fic]—dc22 2007030746

Summary: David and his friends have a new game called Spy Moves, but they never expected to become real-life detectives! When a classmate asks them to solve a case for him, they can't say no. Soon, David and his friends are swept up into a whirlwind of mysteries: Why did the school bully make Tom Chui trade his Sagankiti cards? Did someone sabotage Mr. Chapman's bike? What happened to Kate's cat? And most important of all, does Bonnie Irving like Lee Hall? David and his friends will have to become super spies to crack these mysterious cases.

Art Director: Heather Kindseth
Graphic Designer: Kay Fraser

Photo Credits
Delaney Photography, cover

1 2 3 4 5 6 13 12 11 10 09 08

Printed in the United States of America

Table of Contents

SLOW
EXIT
KEEP OUT
PRIVATE PROPERTY
THE BOOK
SECRET
NOTES
HOME
VISITOR
S
FOR SALE
ORANGE
JUICE
P
GRAPE
ADMIT ONE
KEEP OUT
PRIVATE PROPERTY
EXIT
MEOW
NEON
THE BOOK
SECRET

CHAPTER 1

THE MISSION

The trouble started about a week ago. I was lying under a bush in our local park, just **minding my own business.**

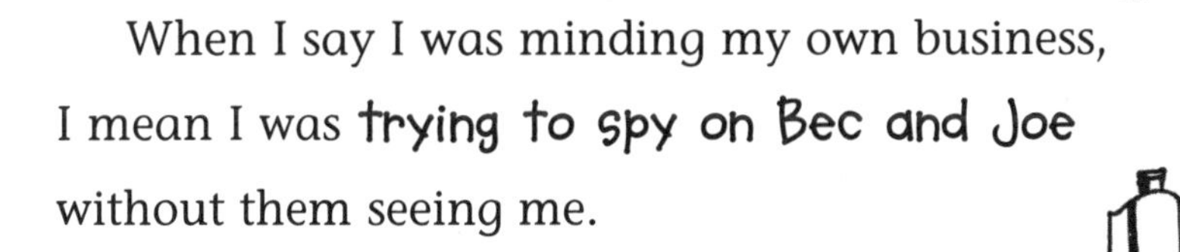

When I say I was minding my own business, I mean I was **trying to spy on Bec and Joe** without them seeing me.

That was okay, because they were doing the same thing to me. And to **each other.**

Anyway, we were all hiding and spying. Then **Jake Davern** came up and tapped me on the shoulder.

I was pretty **SURPRISED** to see him. Jake Davern lived three streets away. He didn't ever hang out on our street.

I grabbed Jake's ankle and pulled him down behind the bush with me. "What are you doing?" I whispered. "You're giving away my position. You're going to get me caught!"

"Hey, David," Jake said. "I heard you were **some kind of detective**."

"I'm not," I said.

"You're not?" said Jake. "So what are you doing now?"

"I'm **SPYING**," I told him.

"Spying?" he asked. **"Like a detective?"**

"Well, okay, yes," I said. I thought I saw a *flash of red* through the trees near the swings, but it disappeared. Maybe I'd imagined it.

"Well, whatever you want to call what you do, I need your help," said Jake.

"Can we talk about this later?" I asked. "I'm kind of **in the middle of something** right now."

"Hey, sure. So, should I like, talk to you at school or something?" Jake asked.

"Yeah," I said. Then I was sure I saw *another flash of red*. I tried to remember what Bec and Joe were wearing. Was Bec wearing her **red coat**? Or maybe Joe was wearing his **red hat.**

"Okay, so, I'll talk to you later," said Jake.

Then the leaves from the bush in front of me moved. **"Caught you!"** It was **Bec**.

"Hey, not fair!" I yelled. "Jake!"

"Hi, Bec," said Jake. He stood up and waved to the tree near the slide. "Hi, Joe."

I heard Joe groan. Jake had just ruined our Spy Moves game.

Spy Moves was a new **Secret Club** game.

Spy Moves Rules

1. The slide was base.
2. You had to get to base (the slide) before anyone saw you.
3. If you saw someone else, you yelled out "Caught you." Then that person was out of the game and had to sit on the slide.
4. If you were out and you saw someone, you could yell out "Spied you." Then you were back in the game and the other person was out.

"Well, I guess we can talk now," I told Jake.

So we sat in the shade of the slide and listened to Jake's problem.

Jake's story was simple enough.

Jake was collecting **Sagankiti** trading cards. Sagankiti was the HOTTEST cartoon on TV. Sagankiti was a karate master and he had a band of followers who fought **evil**. Every week, Sagankiti was faced with new **enemies**.

There were 100 Sagankiti cards to collect. Jake had 99 of them.

There was a contest going on. If you collected all 100 cards, you could send them in and you would be entered to win a trip to Disneyland.

"WOW," said **Joe**. "Just one more and you could win the trip to Disneyland."

"Yeah. I'm just missing the **Purple Pachyderm**," Jake said.

"Why don't you ask Tom?" said Bec. "He collects those cards, doesn't he?"

"He sure does," I said.

Tom Chui collected lots of things. He collected string. He collected rubber bands. He collected action figures. He collected bottle caps and funny bumper stickers and erasers. But **most of all,** he collected **Sagankiti cards.**

"That's the thing," said Jake. "I think he has it."

"So ask him," said Joe.

"I can't," said Jake. "If Tom knows I want that card, he won't want to give it to me. **He thinks collectors should have to hunt for the things they want.** What I need to do is find out what he needs. If I have a double of what he needs, we could trade."

"So you want us to find out for you?" said Bec.

Jake nodded. "*In a hurry,*" he said. "Entries for the Disneyland contest have to be mailed in by this Friday."

I said, "We're going to have to talk this over. Then we'll let you know if we'll take your case."

"What do you think?" I asked Bec and Joe after Jake left. "Should we take Jake's case?"

"I don't know," said Bec. "I mean, we only play spies as a game. **We aren't the real thing.**"

"I think it'd be cool," said Joe. "I have a trench coat at home I can wear!"

"Joe, if we're going **UNDERCOVER**, we don't want to stand out," I said. "I think we're ready. Jake needs us. It's our duty to help him."

"It's a **really cool** trench coat," said Joe. "It has lots of pockets."

"Forget about the trench coat, Joe," I said.

"I'm not sure I want to spy on Tom," said Bec.

"We're not going to spy," I said. "We're just going to ask some **questions**."

"We're not cops," said Bec.

"I know that," I said. I rolled my eyes. Of course we weren't cops. "Anyway," I went on, "this could be good. Tom might just need a card that Jake has. It could be **a win-win situation**."

"Hey, look, it's the LOSERS." The school bully, **Victor Sneddon**, had appeared out of nowhere.

"Are you lost?" I asked. Victor lived at least five blocks away. Sometimes I saw him walking by, though.

He had a CRUSH on my sister, Zoe. I know he was hoping to see her outside one day, but Zoe never left her room.

"I've got a message for your friend," said Victor.

"Jake?" asked Joe.

Victor nodded. "Tell him **Tom Chui** swapped his Sagankiti cards with me for something else he wanted. I only have a couple left to get. Then I'm going to **Disneyland**."

"Tom Chui wouldn't swap his Sagankiti collection for anything," I said. "What did you do to him?"

Victor just smiled. "Let's just say **I made him an offer he couldn't refuse**," he told us.

"Hey, I think I heard that in a movie once," said Joe.

Joe's parents owned the local **video store**. Joe had seen every movie ever made.

Victor **LAUGHED**. Then he walked away.

"I'm ready to take that case," said Bec.

"I think our job just got **a whole lot harder**," I said.

CHAPTER 2

WATCHING THE SUSPECT

The next morning before school we asked Tom about his Sagankiti collection. He told us that he had **traded** his cards with Victor.

"I *wanted* to trade," Tom said.

But I knew he didn't mean it. Victor Sneddon could be pretty SCARY. You didn't want to mess with him. If Victor wanted Tom's cards, Tom wouldn't have a choice about giving them to him.

"Poor Tom," said Bec.

I nodded. "We have to get that collection back to him. Somehow we need to make Victor a better offer."

"Better than **Disneyland?**" asked Joe.

"You mean better than entering a drawing to maybe win a trip to Disneyland," said Bec.

"I think we need to keep an eye on Victor," I said.

"You want us to spy on Victor Sneddon?" asked Joe. **"Are you crazy?"**

"I'm sick of Victor walking around like he's in charge of our school. **Someone's got to do something.** Are you with me?" I asked.

"David, I don't know . . ." said **Bec**.

"I'm with you, David," said Joe.

Bec sighed. Then she nodded. "Okay, I'm in."

The first thing we did was find Jake. We had to tell him that things had changed.

Jake was sitting at his desk. When we told him that Victor had Tom's cards, Jake GROANED. "I guess I should forget the whole thing," he said. "Maybe I was never meant to have that last card."

"That's CRAZY TALK," I said. "We'll find a way to get that card for you. You just have to trust us, Jake."

"How much is this going to cost me?" asked Jake. "I only have a little money left over from my birthday. But I *could pay you later*."

"Who said anything about **money**?" said Bec.

"Although, if you wanted to — **OUCH!**" Joe yelled as Bec punched him in the arm.

"Really, we don't want anything," said Bec. "We're just happy to help."

Then **Ms. Stacey** came into class. She went straight to the whiteboard and wrote **"Volunteer Day."**

"Listen up, class," she said. She waited for us to be quiet. Then she said, "The school's **annual volunteer day** is coming up. We are doing something a little different this year. Each class will be allowed to choose a charity and their own way to raise money."

There was a lot of noise as people started talking. Ms. Stacey held up her hand. "One at a time, please. Raise your hand if you have an idea."

Twenty hands shot up in the air.

Paul wanted to hold a **surfing carnival**, but Ms. Stacey pointed out that we weren't anywhere near the ocean.

Chris said we could hold a **basketball tournament**, but some kids booed because they liked football better.

Stephanie said we could have a **bookworm challenge**, where students raised money by reading as many books as possible in two weeks.

Ms. Stacey wrote the idea on the board and a few people groaned.

Elly said we should try to **trade a paper clip on the Internet** and end up with a house. Then we could donate the house to a charity. Elly said that it **really happened** and that it was on the news, but Ms. Stacey didn't think that would work.

Rose Thornton's face was turning red from keeping her hand up in the air so long. Finally Ms. Stacey asked Rose her idea.

"A talent show, Ms. Stacey," said Rose.

I groaned.

TYPICAL. Rose was always trying to get on stage and show off.

Unfortunately, Ms. Stacey thought it was a good idea.

"How would that work, Rose?" asked Ms. Stacey.

"We could have the competition for the whole school," said Rose. "We could *charge a fee* to everyone who entered the competition. Then we would charge people to come and watch."

Ms. Stacey wrote **"Talent Show"** on the board.

A few more people had ideas and Ms. Stacey put those on the board, too. Then she asked us to vote.

Joe and I voted for the basketball tournament, but **the talent show won.**

I didn't really care. I was too busy thinking about the job I had to do.

* * *

For the rest of the day, the Secret Club followed Victor's every move. We found out that Victor's class was in the library. *That was easy.*

Bec asked Ms. Stacey if she could go to the library to return her late book.

"Yes, but hurry up," said Ms. Stacey.

Bec left with a book. Then, about ten minutes later, she came back with it.

"Isn't the library open?" asked Ms. Stacey.

"What? Oh," Bec looked down at her book. "This is **a different book**."

Then Bec gave Joe and me a nod and sat down at her desk.

I noticed Rose Thornton staring at us, so **I made a face at her**. She looked away.

Then Ms. Stacey asked if someone could go to **Room 4D** and bring back the overhead projector. Joe and I said we'd go. Room 4D was *Victor's classroom.*

We knocked on the door and asked Mr. Jenson for the projector. It was in the back of the room, next to Victor Sneddon's desk.

There on Victor's desk, **in broad daylight**, was Tom's folder of trading cards.

Victor was writing something from the board. With his left hand, he pulled the folder closer to him.

Out in the hallway, I made some more notes in my notebook. Then we went back to class.

At lunchtime, Bec stood in the cafeteria line behind Victor. After Victor got his food, she found Joe and me under the oak tree.

"Got that?" I asked.

Bec nodded and made some notes in her own notebook.

At recess, the three of us played on the basketball court. While we bounced the ball to each other, I *watched Victor*. He was **SHOOTING HOOPS** at the other end of the court.

I let our ball roll to his end of the court. Then I ran to get it. Victor was talking to a guy who was bouncing a **basketball**. The guy just nodded. Victor did all the talking.

I couldn't hear the whole conversation, but I heard the words "**shocks**" and "**wheelset**" and "**double crankset**."

I had *no idea* what these words meant.

When Victor looked over at me, I ran away. I threw the ball to Joe. Then I took my notebook out and wrote down some notes.

After lunch, Ms. Stacey was talking about sharing tasks and everyone **working together** to make the job EASIER.

I wasn't sure what job she was talking about. I was too busy watching Victor.

He was outside, near the bike racks. The bike racks were **off limits** except for before and after school. Victor had walked over to the bike racks, looked around, and then bent over one of the bikes.

Then Joe nudged me.

"Isn't that right, David?" I heard Ms. Stacey say.

I looked at her and said, "Yes, Ms. Stacey."

"So you agree that you should *empty the garbage can* for the rest of the week?" said Ms. Stacey. Someone giggled. I think it was Rose.

No one liked emptying the garbage can. It was filled with DISGUSTING things. Old banana peels. Crusty sandwich crusts. Squashed fruit. There were even brown things that probably hadn't been brown when they started out in lunch boxes.

"Yes, Ms. Stacey," I replied sadly.

"Well, **you can empty our garbage can** now," she said.

All of a sudden this seemed like the best idea in the world.

"Yes, Ms. Stacey," I said one more time.

I grabbed the trashcan from the back of the room and rushed outside.

The large black Dumpster was outside near the equipment shed. The equipment shed was near the bike racks.

I EMPTIED the garbage into the Dumpster. Then I slid behind the equipment shed and looked out at the bike racks.

Victor was still there, looking at the bikes. He seemed very interested in a shiny, black one with a front light and the words "**Race Ace**" in red letters splashed on the side. The bike belonged to Mr. Chapman, the first-grade teacher.

A couple of kids walked out to the equipment shed.

Victor stood up quickly, picked up a folder from the ground, and left. Victor was keeping those trading cards real close.

I thought about him and the bike all the way back to class.

Just before I went inside, I had **an awful thought.**

I knew what Victor had been doing. And I had to tell Mr. Chapman **right away**.

CHAPTER 3

PRIVATE INVESTIGATION

Mr. Chapman's bike had been sabotaged.

I was sure of it. I just wasn't sure how to tell him without Victor finding out.

I told Joe that we needed to have a Secret Club meeting at my house after school.

As soon as the bell RANG, I ran outside to the bike racks. I hung around and waited while other kids came and rode their bikes away.

Finally, Mr. Chapman came outside. "Hello, David," he said cheerfully. **Mr. Chapman was always cheerful.**

"Mr. Chapman, I think you should check the brakes before you ride home," I said.

Mr. Chapman patted me on the shoulder. "Thanks, David. I'll make sure to do that," he said. He started to unlock his bike. He didn't seem to realize that it might have been sabotaged.

“No, really,” I said. “And maybe you should make sure your **wheels** are attached okay. I mean, they might have come loose, since you ride your bike so much.”

“Sure,” said Mr. Chapman. He pulled the lock off of the bike.

“And the handlebars,” I said. “You should make sure they’re screwed on tightly. It would be awful if they were loose, and you lost control of the bike and got hurt or something.”

“David, I take good care of my bike. I keep it in great shape. Now, don’t you worry about a thing,” Mr. Chapman said.

He hopped on his bike and PEDALED away. I watched nervously.

He couldn’t say I didn’t warn him.

By the time I got home, Bec and Joe were already in my kitchen, helping themselves to an afternoon snack.

“Hey, David,” said Joe. “Where have you been?”

I explained to them about Victor and Mr. Chapman's bike. I told them **everything** I'd seen and *everything* I knew.

"David, did you see Victor do something to Mr. Chapman's bike?" asked Bec.

"Well, no. Not really. But he was looking at it for a long time. A really long time. And he was acting STRANGE," I said.

"I think we need to put our notes together," said Bec.

"Notes?" said Joe. "What *notes?*"

"The notes we've been taking about Victor," said Bec.

"Oh. Right. Of course. *Those notes,*" said Joe. "I didn't take notes."

"Joe!" said Bec.

"I don't need to make notes," said Joe. He tapped his head. **"I have it all up here."**

"Okay," I said. "Could you write the stuff in your head down on paper? Then we'll **compare** our data."

This was what we came up with:

Private Investigation Notes from the Secret Club Members

Bec: Entered school library at 9:07 a.m. Suspect (Victor) was in non-fiction section with rest of his class. Class was in library for project research. Upon further investigation, suspect was reading "Go Cycling" magazine.

At 12:14, observed suspect buying three bags of chips and two chocolate bars.

Joe: Suspect had trading card folder on his desk when we picked up the overhead projector from his classroom. Keeps it close at all times.

David: Heard conversation between suspect and Basketball Guy. Check on "shocks," "wheelset," and "double crankset" — what does this mean?

Suspect seen at bike rack after lunch, sabotaging Mr. Chapman's bike. Suspect still had possession of trading card folder.

"You can't say that Victor was sabotaging Mr. Chapman's bike unless you have proof," said Bec. "You just have to report the facts."

"Okay," I said.

David: The suspect was seen at bike racks after lunch. Upon further investigation, the suspect appeared to be interested in Mr. Chapman's bike. Very interested. Extremely interested.

The suspect still had the trading card folder at time of sighting.

We looked over the clues again. This is what we'd learned:

1. **Victor really liked bikes, especially Mr. Chapman's.**
2. **Victor ate a lot of junk food at school.**
3. **Victor was known to leave the classroom during class hours.**
4. **Victor was not letting that trading card folder out of his sight.**
5. **And then there was that conversation with Basketball Guy that didn't make sense. I said I would get back to Bec and Joe after I found out what those words meant.**

Basically, we had NOTHING to go on. Obviously Bec and Joe thought so too, because they looked like they wanted to hand in their detective badges. **Not that we had badges.**

"I think we need **badges**," I said. "Detectives should have badges. You never know. We might need to prove we're GOOD, not EVIL. Just in case someone finds us snooping around."

"Badges," said Joe. "Cool."

"Bec, do you think you can design something?" I asked. Bec is a **really** good artist.

"Of course I can," said Bec. "But what is the point of badges?"

"We need to be professional about this," I told her.

Then I had another great idea.

"From now on, we'll be known as **The Secret Club Detective Agency.** And we'll be secret," I told them.

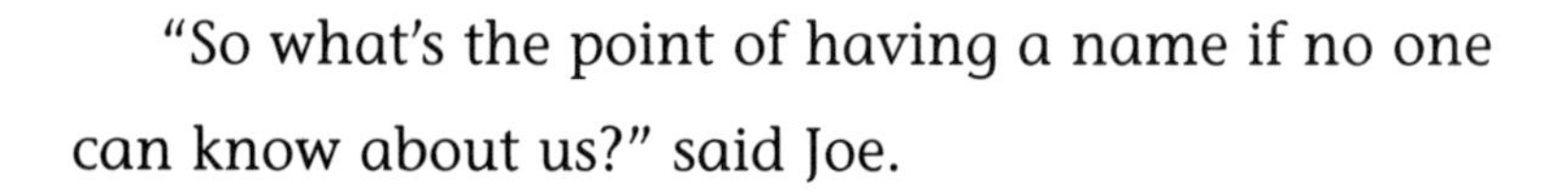

"So what's the point of having a name if no one can know about us?" said Joe.

"Joe, they may not know about us, but *they need us*," I said. "People like Jake Davern. People like Tom Chui. Even people like Mr. Chapman. People who need to know that **good will always win over evil**. That truth will always win over lies. That trading cards belong to their owners and should not be stolen by **BULLIES** like Victor Sneddon."

"Wow," said Joe. "I got **goosebumps** listening to that."

"Yeah, me too," I said.

CHAPTER 4

BLOWING OUR COVER

The next day I asked Mr. Chapman how his trip home was. He said **his bike was still okay.**

Bec said that proved that Victor hadn't sabotaged Mr. Chapman's bike. I thought that maybe it just proved that Victor **ran out of time** to do whatever he'd been planning to do.

I'd looked up the words I'd overheard on the basketball court the day before — **shocks, wheelset, and double crankset.** I found all three words on a website that sold bicycle parts.

My *brilliant detective's mind* had spotted a pattern in all the clues.

Victor was **OBSESSED** with bikes.

I just didn't see how that tied into the trading card collection. But maybe it didn't need to. Or maybe I was missing something.

I had a meeting with Jake at recess.

I filled him in on the investigation so far.

"Thanks for **everything** you're doing," said Jake.

"It's nothing," I said. "But remember, the Secret Club Detective Agency is a secret. You can't discuss this case with anyone."

"Oh. Okay," said Jake.

"I'm serious, Jake," I said. **"Loose lips sink ships."**

"Don't worry," said Jake. "Your secret is **SAFE** with me."

At lunchtime, Kate was looking for me. I knew that because a couple of kids said, "Kate is looking for you."

I told them she could find me under the oak tree with Joe and Bec if she wanted me.

I wondered what she wanted. Kate was one of Rose's friends.

Rose Thornton, the person I like the least in the whole world.

Rose Thornton, cousin of Victor Sneddon.

Joe and Bec and I were talking Secret Club business when **Kate** walked over.

"Hello," she said. "I hear that you're detectives."

"Where did you hear that?" I asked.

"Jake Davern," she said.

I banged my fist on the ground. **Jake was going to blow our cover.**

"He's wrong," I said. "Sorry."

Kate looked sad. "That's too bad," she said. "I need HELP."

She told us that her **cat** had been missing for two days. It had **never** been missing before. Kate looked at the ground and kicked at the dirt.

"Whiskers is such a good cat," she said. "I got him last Christmas and now we won't be able to spend another Christmas together." She looked like she was going to cry.

"We'll help you," I said. I hate it when girls cry. "Not that I'm saying we're **detectives,** but we could still help you," I added.

Bec and Joe looked at me like I was crazy.

"Won't we?" I said.

"Sure," said Bec.

"Yeah, okay," said Joe.

I whipped out my handy notebook from my back pocket. **A good detective** should always have a notebook to take notes in.

"Start from the beginning," I told Kate. "From the time the cat went missing until now. And you'll have to give us a full description of what he looks like."

* * *

At the end of lunchtime, I found Jake and asked him why he'd BLABBED about our detective agency.

"You didn't tell me to keep it a secret until after I told Kate," said Jake.

You couldn't argue with that.

"Well, just as long as you didn't tell anyone else," I said.

Jake shook his head. "No one else."

"Great," I said.

"I'm pretty sure," Jake added.

"What?" I asked.

"I said, I'm pretty sure I haven't told anyone else. Maybe just one other person, but that's **definitely** it."

"Jake!" I yelled.

But it was too late. The bell rang and Jake had already run back inside.

* * *

By the end of the day, the Secret Club Detective Agency had three jobs.

Our **first** was Jake's trading card problem. The **second** case was finding the missing cat, Whiskers. And the **third** case was for Lee Hall. He wanted to know if Bonnie Irvine liked him.

Joe, Bec, and I met under the oak tree after school. I decided the Secret Club Detective Agency needed to **get smart** about its work.

"We need to divide the jobs up," I said. "There's no point in us all working on the same problem."

"Okay," said Bec. "I'll work on the missing Whiskers case."

"I'll take the Lee Hall case," said Joe.

Great. I'd been hoping to give Jake's case to someone else.

"I guess I'm on Jake's case then," I said. "How are those **badge designs** going, Bec?"

Bec said, "I was working on them last night. **I have a couple of ideas.** But now I'm going to be too busy just doing my homework and finding clues on the missing cat."

"Your case shouldn't take too long, Joe," I said. "When you finish you can help me."

Joe frowned. "I don't know, David," he said. "**Who-likes-who stuff** can take a really long time."

"Fine," I said.

I knew Jake's case was the hardest, but **I was the best man for the job.** "Let's report back after school tomorrow and see what we've come up with," I told Bec and Joe.

I watched Victor Sneddon leave through the front gate. He had his backpack slung over one shoulder. I could see the folder of **trading cards** poking out from his backpack.

"I've got to look in that folder," I muttered. "But how?"

"Maybe I can help you," a voice said.

Someone was standing behind us listening in.

It was Rose Thornton.

CHAPTER 5

ROSE HELPS

"How long have you been standing there?" I asked.

"Long enough," said Rose.

"Why would you help us?" demanded Joe.

"Maybe I'm just a nice person," said Rose.

Bec SNORTED.

"Maybe there's something you can help me with. I help you, you help me," said Rose. "I hear you're running some kind of **detective** agency."

"Is there anyone Jake hasn't told?" I muttered.

"You shouldn't **blame** Jake," said Rose. "Kate told me."

"Why should we trust you, Rose?" Bec asked.

Rose shrugged. "If you don't want my help . . ." She turned away.

"No, wait!" I said. **I sighed.** "We do want your help, Rose." I hated to admit it, but it was true.

"Fine. Come to my place at six o'clock tonight," said Rose. Then she walked away.

"What does **SHE** want help with?" asked Joe.

I shook my head. "I don't have any idea," I said. I didn't trust Rose. **Not one bit.** But I really wanted to look at that trading card folder. Time was running out for the Disneyland competition.

"I'm going to go to Rose's," I said. "There are only **four days left** for Jake to get that entry in for the Disneyland competition. I need to check it out, even if Rose is just setting me up. So who's coming?"

"Too busy," said Bec.

Joe nodded. "Me too."

"Fine," I said. "I'll go alone."

I didn't need them anyway.

I could do this job standing on my head.

* * *

At six o'clock I knocked on Rose's front door. Rose pulled me inside.

"Hurry up," she said. "*Before my mother—*"

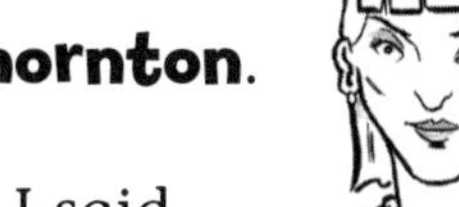

“David!” It was **Mrs. Thornton**.

“Hello, Mrs. Thornton,” I said.

My parents and Rose’s parents are friends. The kind of friends that eat dinner together sometimes at each other’s houses. The kind of friends that call when it’s your birthday.

The kind of friends that think **their kids should be friends.**

Mrs. Thornton was always nice to me, even though she talked to me like I might be DEAF or maybe a little stupid.

“How are your parents, David?” she asked loudly.

“Good, thanks,” I said.

“And your grandmother?”

“Yep, good.”

“And how’s your brother?” Mrs. Thornton asked.

“Yes, his whole family’s fine, Mother,” said Rose. “David and I have some homework to do.”

Rose pushed me up the stairs into her room. She closed the door. Then she pulled Tom's trading card folder out of a large plastic bag. She put it on her desk.

"You've got **twenty minutes**," she said. "Victor will be back from visiting his sister then. His family's here for dinner. He was going to take the folder with him, but **I said I'd take care of it.**"

I pulled my notebook out of my pocket and grabbed the folder.

I checked my notes.

Missing card — Purple Pachyderm.

Inside the folder there were plastic sleeves with pockets to slide your cards into. I **QUICKLY** flicked through the sheets.

No **Purple Pachyderm** card anywhere.

I flicked through again, slowly this time, and found it on the second to last sheet.

The **Purple Pachyderm, card number 78.** There were two Purple Pachyderms, so I took one.

I looked through the sheets one more time. There were two spaces where cards were MISSING.

Number 34 and number 12 were both missing. I jotted this down in my notebook.

"Rose?" It was Victor's voice. We heard footsteps coming up the stairs.

"Oh no!" whispered Rose. **"Hide!"**

But there was nowhere to hide. I looked around the room.

"Rose?" Victor called out again.

I crawled under the desk. Then, two seconds later, the door opened.

"Didn't you hear me calling you?" **Victor growled**. "What are you doing with my book?"

Then I got really scared. We hadn't had time to put the book away.

Victor was going to find me.

He was going to find me and kill me.

I didn't think Rose was going to come to my rescue.

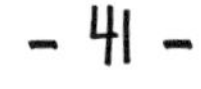

“I was just looking at it,” said Rose.

“I told you not to touch it,” said Victor.

“It's just a bunch of cards,” said Rose. “It's pretty DUMB, if you ask me.”

“No one's asking you, Rose,” Victor said.

I heard the folder snap shut.

“You know why that book's so important,” said Victor.

“I told you my mom would pay,” Rose whispered.

Victor banged the desktop. The noise made my ears ring. Then he said, “I want to do this. I need to do this by myself, Rose. I already told you that.”

Then Victor left the room. Rose said, “David, you're going to have to *sneak out*. I'll try to keep him out of your way.”

It took me five minutes to get out of the house without anyone seeing me.

I had to use all my Secret Club spying skills, but I finally managed to get through the front door.

Before I closed the door, I heard Mrs. Thornton say, "Make sure you say hi to your folks, David."

I ran. **I didn't stop until I got home.**

CHAPTER 6

A WIN-WIN SITUATION

I called Jake when I got home and told him the good news.

"You've got the **Purple Pachyderm**?" he asked. Then he whooped into the phone for five minutes.

I said, "You still have time to send this off to the competition. So tell me how that works again?"

Jake explained that each **complete set of Sagankiti trading cards** needed to be sent into the Sagankiti headquarters.

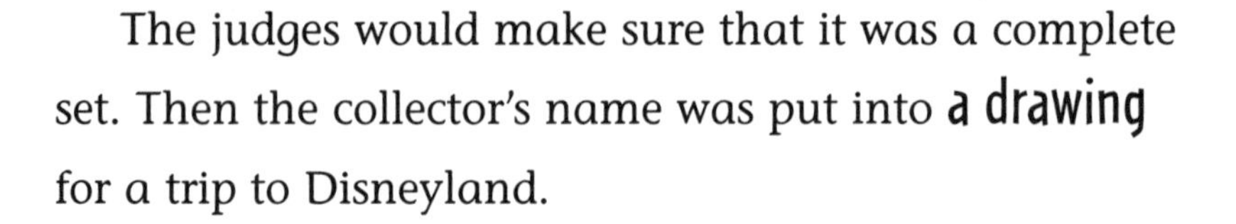

The judges would make sure that it was a complete set. Then the collector's name was put into **a drawing** for a trip to Disneyland.

"So you get to go to Disneyland by yourself?" I asked.

"And a parent or guardian," said Jake.

He said he was coming over to get the card. Then he'd get his dad to send the folder the next day.

I called **Bec** to tell her the good news. She didn't seem that happy.

"So you **STOLE** the card?" she asked.

"Well, yeah," I said. "He had another one, anyway."

"What about the **win-win** idea?" said Bec. "Didn't Victor have some cards missing? Couldn't Jake trade the **Purple Pachyderm** for something else?"

"What are you saying?" I asked.

"I'm saying you need to go back to Victor and tell him," Bec told me.

"*Victor will kill me*," I said. "There's no way I can do that. Anyway, Victor won't want to trade. He just wants the last two missing cards. **He's not going to help Jake win.** Victor *really* wants to win that trip, Bec. I'm not sure why, but he does."

Then we talked about **Whiskers**, the missing cat. Bec had made some posters and put them around the neighborhood. She was planning on putting some up at school too.

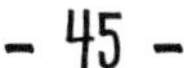

"I interviewed Kate's whole family, but I didn't get anywhere," said Bec. "I took notes, though. Maybe we should have a meeting."

"I'll call Joe," I said. "Let's have the meeting after school tomorrow."

I heard the **doorbell ring**, so I told Bec I had to go.

When I got to the front door, Jake yelled, "Where's the card, David? Where's the **Purple Pachyderm**?"

I thought about Bec.

Maybe she was right. Maybe it was wrong of me to take the Purple Pachyderm without talking to Victor first.

"I can't actually give it to you yet," I said.

"What?" **Jake looked shocked.**

"Do you have your collection with you?" I asked.

"Of course," said Jake. He pulled it out of his backpack.

I pulled my notebook out of my pocket and checked my notes.

Jake had three number 34 cards and two number 12 cards.

Those were the cards that **Victor still needed.**

I made Jake leave the cards with me. I promised to let him know as soon as I could give him the Purple Pachyderm.

"There isn't much time left," Jake complained as I shut the door in his face.

Running a detective agency was pretty tiring. I didn't want to do anything that night except watch Smashing Smorgan on *Wrestling Mania.* **But the phone kept ringing.**

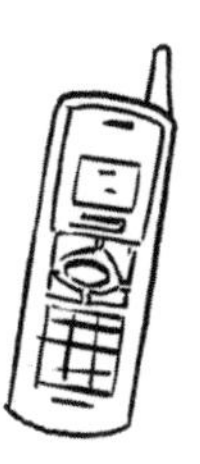

The first time the phone rang, it was Joe to say that he thought he had his case wrapped up.

"I don't think Lee's going to be happy with what I found out," said Joe.

"Well, **it's not our job to change the truth,**" I said. "We just have to report it."

Halfway through Smashing Smorgan's match, Bec called to report on the case of the missing cat.

I told my brother *I didn't want to talk at the moment*, so **Harry** said, "He doesn't want to talk to you, Bec."

I grabbed the phone from him.

"You tell him that if he thinks—" Bec was saying.

"Hi Bec," I said. "Sorry about that. Harry gets things mixed up sometimes."

So then Bec told me all about her missing cat case. There had been a few sightings, and a few leads that went nowhere.

By the time we finished talking, **Smashing Smorgan** was raising his fist in VICTORY.

I had missed the whole match.

"Great!" I said.

I went to the kitchen and grabbed the chocolate ice cream from the freezer.

I filled a bowl to the top and sat at the counter, eating it in the dark.

Then Dad turned the light on. "David! I thought you were in bed," he said. He filled a glass with water.

"Nope," I said.

"What's going on?" Dad asked.

"Nothing," I said.

"Things have a way of working themselves out," said Dad. "Especially after a good night's sleep. And you can always talk to me."

I nodded. "Thanks, Dad."

I knew what I had to do.

I grabbed the cordless phone and Mom's telephone book and took them to my room.

Boris, my faithful dog, followed me in. Then I shut the door.

I dialed the Thorntons' phone number. Mrs. Thornton answered.

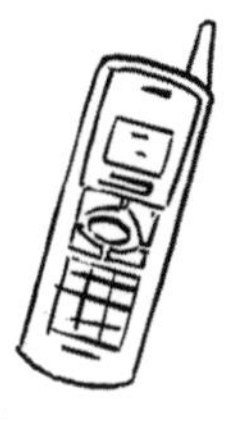

"Oh, it's you, David," she said loudly. I had to hold the phone away from my ear. "I was just saying to Rose, who could that be calling so late. **Is everything all right?"** Mrs. Thornton asked.

"Sorry to call so late, Mrs. Thornton," I said. "But I really need to speak to Rose. It's about that **homework project** we were doing after school."

Rose got on the phone. "What do you want, David Baxter?" she asked.

"I took one of Victor's cards," I said quickly. "Today, when I was at your house."

"What!" said Rose. **"Are you crazy**, David? When he finds out one of those cards is—"

"I want you to tell him," I said. "Here's the deal. I already have the card I want from him. He has two cards missing and I'm willing to give them to him. Then we're even."

I explained my plan to Rose.

I would put the cards in a plastic bag. Then I would tape them behind the water pipe in the last stall in the boys' bathroom at school.

"Tell Victor that it's **the stall where the paint on the back of the door peeled off in the shape of a dog's head,"** I told Rose. "He'll know the one I mean."

"Okay," said Rose. "Wait a second. What do you get out of this?"

"It's the right thing to do," I said. "Then **both Victor and Jake will have a shot at winning the trip to Disneyland.** Not that Victor deserves it. I don't know how he got those cards from **Tom Chui** but I know that Tom wouldn't have given up those cards **if he had a choice.**"

"Why do you always think the worst of Victor?" asked Rose. "Maybe it was a **fair trade.** Maybe he has his own reasons for wanting to win the trip. Did you ever think of that, David Baxter?"

"Can you just tell him?" I asked. "But give me until **8:30** tomorrow morning. Then everything will be set in place for the drop off."

"Okay," said Rose.

"And Rose?" I added. "You still haven't told me what job you want us to do for **YOU.**"

"That's okay," said Rose. "It's not the right time yet. I'll tell you later."

Then she hung up.

I could hardly sleep that night. I was too WORRIED about what I had to do.

And I couldn't stop wondering **What Rose Thornton wanted** in return for her help.

CHAPTER 7

THE DROP

The next morning I snuck out of the house with a plastic bag, a roll of sticky tape, and the two cards all **hidden in my lunch box.** Jake's card collection was in my backpack.

At school, I taped the cards in place. Then I hid in an empty classroom next to the bathroom.

About ten minutes later, I saw Victor RUSH into the bathroom. Soon, he came out with the plastic bag in his hand. He looked both ways and then took off down the hall.

"That's taken care of," I muttered.

In class, Rose walked past me. I nodded at her. She nodded back.

Bec frowned at me. I hadn't had a chance to tell her or Joe what was going on.

I went over to the pencil sharpener near Jake and told him **everything was taken care of.**

"Hey, that's great, David. Thanks for everything," **Jake** said.

I just waved my pencil at him. **"Nothing we couldn't handle,"** I said.

"So where's my folder?" he asked.

"In my locker," I said. "I'll give it to you at recess."

* * *

But at recess the folder wasn't there. I searched my locker and my backpack about fifty times. **I broke out into a cold sweat.**

Jake was behind me, hopping from one foot to the other. "Where is it, David?" he asked.

I wasn't sure what to tell him. Maybe this was a situation for the truth. "I don't seem to have it," I said.

"What?" Jake stopped hopping. "Tell me what's going on. How did you get that extra card?"

So I told him. **I told him everything.**

"Now Victor has a chance to win, but I don't," wailed Jake. "The cards are gone. What are you going to do?"

I shook my head. "I don't know, Jake," I said sadly.

"Thanks for nothing," said Jake. Then he walked away.

I felt sick.

When I found Bec and Joe under the oak tree, Bec said, "Victor. Victor took it."

"But why would he?" I asked. "He already has all of the cards."

"Jake's his competition," said Bec. "Victor has a better chance of winning **if Jake isn't in the picture.** You're going to have to ask Victor."

"You want me to walk up to Victor Sneddon and ask him why he took Jake's folder out of my locker?" I asked.

"Yep," said Joe.

"Well, if you think that's **such a good idea,** why don't you do it?" I said to Joe.

"It's not my case," said Joe.

"And what about your case?" I asked. "Did you tell Lee what's going on?"

Joe looked NERVOUS. "I haven't gotten around to that," he said.

"To what?" said Bec.

"Telling Lee that Bonnie Irvine **doesn't like him,"** Joe told her.

"Who said?" demanded Bec.

"Bonnie Irvine," said Joe.

"What?" Bec said. She shook her head. "Don't tell me you just went up to Bonnie Irvine and asked her whether she liked Lee Hall. Is that how you cracked the case, Joe?"

Joe looked **confused.** "How else would I find out?" he asked.

"That's it," said Bec. "I'm trading cases with Joe. Joe, I'll explain to you what's going on with the missing cat. It shouldn't take long to give you all of the details. Then, after school, I'll start work on **finding out if Bonnie really does like Lee** or not."

"But I already asked her," Joe said.

Bec rolled her eyes. "Joe, **no girl is going to tell you that she likes another boy** if you ask her. You have to be more **subtle**. Do you even know what **subtle** means, Joe?"

"Sure I do," said Joe.

I was pretty sure that Joe did not know what that word meant. (One time Bec said the same thing to me. She said, "David, you have to be more subtle. Do you even know what subtle means, David?" I told her that I did, but I didn't. When I got home I asked Dad, and he told me it meant careful and clever, like not just going up to Bonnie and asking her if she liked Lee. If you were being subtle, you'd say something like "So, Bonnie, how are you?" and then you'd have to ask a million questions to find out if she liked Lee.)

Anyway, there was no way Joe knew what **subtle** meant.

I tried to change the subject. "Well, what about my case?" I asked. "And where are our **badges**, Bec?"

Bec frowned at me. "David, I've been **BUSY.** If you're so **WORRIED** about badges, why don't you make them?" Bec said. Then she stormed off.

Joe looked and me and shrugged. "So, are you going to talk to Victor, David? Do you want me to come with you?" he asked.

I shook my head. "Sounds like you're looking for a missing cat," I said. "But thanks anyway."

I walked over to the basketball courts. Victor was playing one on one with the Basketball Guy. Victor saw me watching, **faked** a move, and then walked over. "Hey," he said.

"Hey," I said.

"I got those cards," Victor said.

I nodded.

"So we're even," he said. "And **may the best man win** and all that." He bounced the ball once and caught it with one hand.

"So why did you take Jake's cards from my locker?" I finally blurted out.

"What are you talking about?" Victor asked.

"Jake's cards," I said. "They were in my locker this morning and now they aren't."

"You think I took them?" Victor's lips were twisted in a strange smile. "Your **stupid cards** are gone so you think I took them? Why would I need to? I already have my own. And this afternoon I'm sending them to the contest," he told me.

"Well, it's obvious. You did it because you wanted to knock out your competition," I said. "You didn't want Jake to be up against you in the drawing. One less person . . ."

I stopped talking. Victor looked really STRANGE. He had **a weird smile** on his face but he wasn't happy and he wasn't being mean.

Actually, *he looked like he might cry.*

"Well, you have it all figured out, don't you?" he asked.

I nodded. But all of a sudden, I wasn't so sure that I did have it figured out.

"Feel free to check my locker," he said. "I don't have the stupid cards. Now get out of my face before I hurt you."

I ran away as quick as I could.

The worst thing was, **I believed him.**

But the cards were still missing and Jake was running out of time.

CHAPTER 8

THE SECRET CLUB DETECTIVE AGENCY

"So, why would a cat **disappear?"** asked Joe for the third time.

We were sitting at the kitchen table after school that day. Joe was dunking one of Mom's homemade cookies into a tall glass of cold milk.

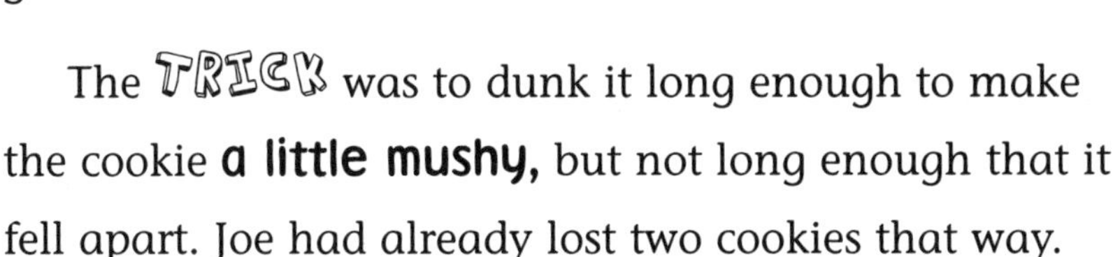

The **TRICK** was to dunk it long enough to make the cookie **a little mushy,** but not long enough that it fell apart. Joe had already lost two cookies that way.

"I don't know," I said. I was too busy wondering about Jake's cards.

Joe, Bec, and I had looked everywhere after school. We searched the whole school, even the bathrooms, but **no cards.**

"Are you sure you had it in your backpack?" asked Bec.

I nodded.

"What? The cat?" said Joe.

"The card folder," said Bec.

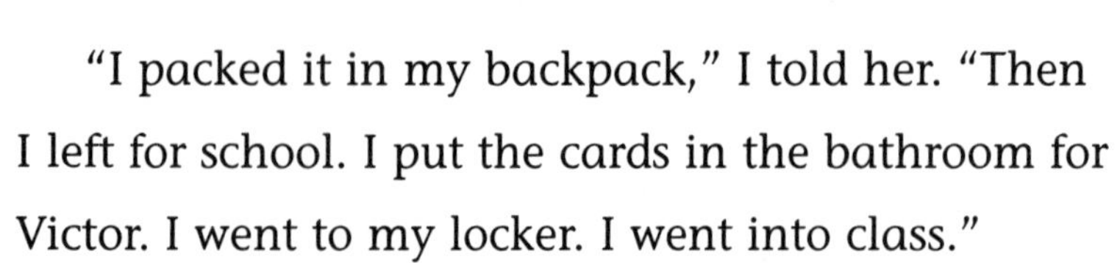

"I packed it in my backpack," I told her. "Then I left for school. I put the cards in the bathroom for Victor. I went to my locker. I went into class."

"I think we need to retrace your footsteps," said Bec. "Like those shows on TV do."

"Hey, that's a good idea," said Joe.

"Well, I just want to say that **I solved my case,"** said Bec smugly.

"You did?" said Joe.

"I was able to report back to our client, Lee Hall, and give him the information he **needed to know,"** Bec told us.

"Which was what?" I asked.

Bec tapped her nose. "Sorry, boys," she said in a **SNEAKY** voice. "That's **personal,** and it's between me and my client. I can't tell you. Anyway, that frees me up to help someone else with their case. Who should it be?"

"Me," said Joe.

"Wait," I said, holding up my hand. "I've been thinking about this. The Secret Club has always been the three of us, right? **That's what makes it fun.** Ever since we started the Secret Club Detective Agency, we've been going our own ways. And it just isn't working."

"Actually, I solved my case," said Bec.

"Yeah, well, other than that, it just hasn't been working," I said. "I think we are STRONGER if we stick together. What do you say?"

"So we should all work on Jake's case together?" asked Joe.

"Yep, and we should all find the **missing cat,**" I explained.

"Okay," said Bec.

"Cool," said Joe.

"This is what I think we should do," I said. "Meet me here *first thing tomorrow morning*. We'll see if we can find the cards. Then, after school, we'll spend time looking for the cat. Agreed?"

The others nodded. Then we did **our secret handshake** to seal the deal.

It was good to be a team again.

* * *

The next morning, Joe and Bec met me in my front yard. I had a folder shoved into my backpack. It was about the same size as Jake's missing card folder.

"Okay," said Bec. "Joe and I will walk behind you and observe. You just do everything you did yesterday morning. Just forget we're here."

I walked to school, listening to Joe and Bec talking behind me.

At school, I went into the boys' bathroom and went to the last stall, with the peeling paint door.

Bec didn't follow me in, but Joe was right behind me. I **pretended** to tape the cards onto the water pipe. Then I walked out of the bathroom and went to the empty classroom next door.

Joe followed me. "Where are you going now?" he asked.

"I **hid** here and watched to see if Victor would turn up," I said.

Then Bec tapped me on the shoulder.

"TA-DA!" she said. She was holding Jake's folder.

"It must have slipped out of my bag when I was waiting for Victor," I said. I opened it up and looked inside. Everything seemed to be there.

"You did it," said Joe.

"We did it," I said. "Let's go tell Jake."

We found Jake on the playground. Bec handed him the folder.

"COOL," Jake said. "But it's too late. The contest ends tomorrow. It won't get there on time if I send it now."

"That's why we have to take it there," I said. "We have to deliver it ourselves."

"How?" asked Jake.

"I bet my mom would take us. If I said it was an **emergency,** she definitely would. And it is an **emergency,** Jake," I said.

"You're the **best**, David," said Jake.

"I'm going to have to ask Rose Thornton if I can use her cell phone," I said. "But first I have to talk to Victor Sneddon. I owe him an apology."

"We're coming with you," said Bec.

We found Victor looking around the bike rack. Tom Chui had just ridden up on his new bike and was padlocking it. Victor was checking out the tires and giving Tom some advice.

"Hey, Victor," I called out.

Victor stood still and waited for us to come over. His eyebrows were hanging over his eyes like a thundercloud. I could tell he wanted to hit me, so I kept out of reach.

"Victor, I owe you an APOLOGY," I said.

"What?" Victor asked. He looked shocked.

"I'm sorry. About saying you'd stolen Jake's cards. I found them. So I'm sorry," I told him.

Victor relaxed a little. He GRUNTED.

"So did you mail your cards already?" I asked.

Victor shook his head. Then he said, "No."

"But the contest ends tomorrow," I said.

"Look, it's been too hard. **You don't understand,"** said Victor. He started walking away.

"**WAIT!**" I said. "We'll take you. After school. We're going to drop Jake's cards off at the contest headquarters. Meet us at my place."

Victor turned around. He looked like he thought we might be tricking him.

"Why would you do that?" he asked.

"Hey, may the best man win and all that," I said. "So are you coming?"

"Maybe," he said. Then he walked away.

Joe was over at the bike racks looking at Tom's new bike. Tom explained that actually it wasn't a new bike, just new for him.

"So where did you get it?" asked Bec.

"It was Victor's," said Tom. "He traded it for my trading card collection."

"What?" I couldn't believe it.

Victor swapped a bike for a chance to win a trip to Disneyland?

"Why would he do that?" I asked.

Tom shrugged. "He said **he had his reasons**. I'm not really into bikes. You can tell Victor was really into bikes. I mean, **he loved this bike.** I think he kept it in his room at night. It doesn't have a scratch on it."

"Okay, that's just strange," said Bec.

I nodded. "We're missing some information. We don't have all the clues. **There's something going on with Victor.** And I'm going to find out what it is."

CHAPTER 9

THE DEADLINE

At recess, I asked Rose if I could use her cell phone to call my mom. I said it was an emergency. She said if it was an emergency, **I should use the office phone.**

I said, "Look, Rose, I just need to use your phone. I can pay you. TOMORROW."

Rose sighed. She reached into her pocket, pulled out her pink phone, and handed it to me. I punched in our home number.

Mom picked up after the third ring. I told Mom the whole story, kind of.

Finally, she said, "Okay, okay. I'll take you into the city. But we'll need to leave at four on the dot. The traffic is **terrible** at that time of day."

"You're the best, Mom," I said. I hung up.

"Thanks," I said to Rose. I handed her the phone.

"Whatever," Rose said.

"Now I need to ask you about your cousin," I told her.

Rose raised her eyebrows. "I don't know what you mean," she said. But I could tell she did.

"Rose, what's going on with Victor?" I asked.

Rose made the **annoying little clicking sound** with her tongue that she does when she's thinking. Then she seemed to make a decision. "Okay, I'll tell you," she said.

* * *

At four o'clock there was a **PROBLEM.**

There was only one car and too many people.

Rose said she wanted to go because I had used her phone and she **deserved** to go.

Of course, Joe and Bec wanted to go. So did Jake, who was holding onto his folder like it might disappear at any moment.

Then Victor walked up, and **Mom made a decision.** "Okay," Mom said. "Whose cards are we taking to the city? Hands up."

Victor and Jake both raised their hands.

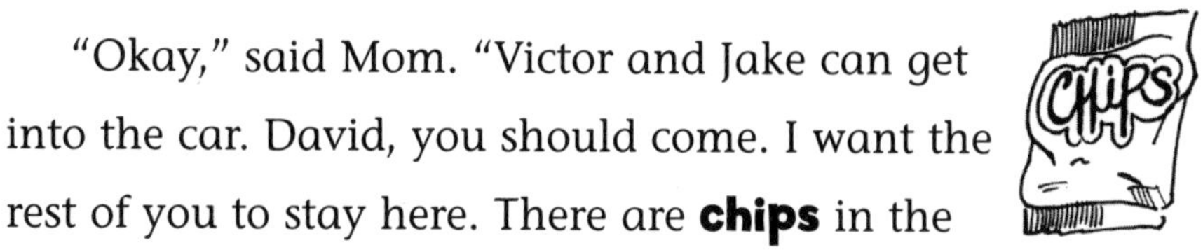

"Okay," said Mom. "Victor and Jake can get into the car. David, you should come. I want the rest of you to stay here. There are **chips** in the pantry, **milk** in the fridge, and a **TV** in the living room. Get COMFORTABLE and wait if you want. We'll be back soon."

"Hey, maybe you could work on that Whiskers case," I mentioned to Joe and Bec as I got into the car.

"What's the Whiskers case?" I heard Rose say as we drove away.

The traffic wasn't too bad until we got into the city. **Then we had to find a place to park.** Mom found a spot a couple of blocks away from where the contest office was.

She looked at her watch. "Let's **hurry**," she said.

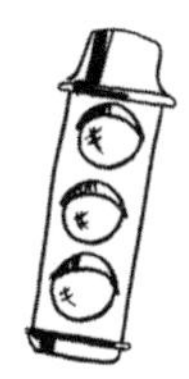

We ran. The only time we stopped running was when we stopped for the traffic lights. By the time we got to the office building, we only had five minutes to spare. We ran up to the door.

But the door was locked.

There were no lights on in the building. Victor rattled the door until Jake said, "What's this?"

There was a large notice on the door. Apparently the Fumi Corporation, makers of the Sagankiti cartoon and cards, had declared **bankruptcy.**

"What's that?" asked Jake.

"It means **they don't have any money,**" said Mom. **"They have gone out of business."**

"But what about the contest?" asked Jake. "What about the trip?"

Mom shook her head.

Victor was still pounding on the doors. **"Let us in! Let us in!"** he shouted.

Mom patted his shoulder. "I'm sorry, Victor," she said quietly. "Let's go."

"But I have to win that trip. **You don't understand,**" Victor said. I thought he was going to cry.

So I did something I had never done before. I stepped up to Victor and looked him in the eye.

"I know," I said. "I know about your sister. **She's sick.** I know you wanted to win the Disneyland trip for her. Well, we're just going to have to give her that trip another way," I said.

* * *

When we got home, Victor said thanks to my mom and threw the Sagankiti folder on the ground.

"See ya," he said as he walked off.

I picked up the folder. Bec rushed out to us.

"We found the cat!" she said. "We found Whiskers. It's AMAZING. I was talking to Rose . . . David, what's wrong?"

Inside, everyone was waiting to hear our story. It wasn't the story they expected to hear.

"This is unfair," said Jake. "Isn't it illegal?"

"A lot of people must have lost their jobs," said Mom. "I'm sure they're feeling **much worse** than we are."

My sister, Zoe, came into the living room and turned on the news.

The man on the news was saying that the Fumi Corporation had lost a lot of money in a bad investment. It was a **really big deal.**

"Where's Victor?" asked Rose.

"He left," I said.

"He did that all for NOTHING," said Rose, shaking her head. "He traded his bike for those cards."

"So that he could send his sister to Disneyland," I said.

CHAPTER 10

THE WHO'S GOT TALENT SHOW

"What's blue and has big ears? An elephant at the North Pole!" After I told the punch line, I pointed to Luke Firth, who did a drum roll.

"Thank you very much," I said as a few people clapped. "Now, for your entertainment pleasure, I present to you Jake Davern, who will be performing his animal act."

I clapped as **Jake** walked out to the microphone. Then I moved backstage.

When *the class voted for me* to be the announcer for the Who's Got Talent Show, **Ms. Stacey** didn't look happy. She made me promise that I would do the job properly, and I said I would.

But that didn't mean I couldn't add in some jokes to keep things interesting.

I peeked out at the audience. The school gym was **PACKED.**

There were even people standing up at the back because there weren't enough seats. Once the word had gotten out, everyone in town wanted to come to our **talent show.**

I watched Jake walk off stage after his act. Then I ran forward to the microphone.

"Let's hear it for Jake Davern," I said, and people clapped. **"What do you call an elephant that flies?"**

"Dumbo," someone yelled out from the audience.

"No, **a jumbo jet!**" I answered.

Luke did his drum roll.

"Now here's Rudy Savoia with his magic show, the Trick of Doom," I said.

Backstage, Rose was doing her voice exercises.

Bec was busy talking to Kate, and Joe was talking to Ms. Stacey.

Someone put a heavy hand on my shoulder.

I turned to see **Victor Sneddon** LOOMING over me.

"It's a good show," he said.

I nodded.

"THANKS," he said.

* * *

Did you know that people will pay money for just about **anything?**

Once the Fumi Corporation had closed down, the Sagankiti cards were more **popular** with collectors than ever.

Zoe sold Jake and Victor's cards on the Internet and ended up with a ton of money.

Jake said he wanted the money to go to Victor's sister. Victor wasn't going to take it until Zoe said that **he should just take it and be quiet.**

So we had that money, and the money raised by our talent show at school. All together, **we managed to raise enough money for Victor's sister to go to Disneyland with her mom.**

It turned out that **Whiskers** wasn't missing at all. She'd had some kittens in a shed near Kate's garden.

It was Rose's idea to look there, because that's what her cat had done **when it had kittens.** Kate offered Bec a kitten as a reward, but Bec didn't think her pet rat would be happy about that.

Bonnie Irvine did like Lee Hall. You could tell by the way they traded lunches at lunchtime.

Victor Sneddon was saving up to buy another bike. He was doing extra jobs like **washing cars** and **walking dogs** and **being a bodyguard for the nerdy kids.** Actually, he wasn't doing that last thing, even though I suggested it.

* * *

About a week after the talent show, Joe, Bec, and I were sitting in the park.

"Oh, I almost FORGOT," said Bec. She pulled something out of her coat pocket. "I guess it's kind of **late** for these."

Bec had made some detective badges for us.

In the middle of the badge was a rat. Circling the rat were the words **Secret Club Detective Agency.**

"Hey, these are cool," said Joe. "Too bad we'll never use them."

"Who knows?" Bec asked. "And we still have a job to do, you know. I finally found out what Rose Thornton wanted us to do."

"You did?" I asked.

Bec nodded. "She's been trying to track down a special sparkly collar for her dog that she saw on TV a couple of weeks ago," she explained.

"What?" said Joe.

"What?" I said. "You have got to be JOKING. We're a **detective** agency. Not a dog-grooming agency."

"But you promised you'd help Rose," said Bec.

"Well, why should we?" asked Joe.

"Because Rose helped us with the trading card mystery," Bec said.

"Oh," said Joe. "Well, then, I guess we have to help her."

"I hate Rose Thornton," I said.

"Remember what your mother says about that word," warned Bec.

"Okay, I really really really don't like Rose Thornton," I said.

But I knew I would help her.

Being part of the Secret Club Detective Agency wasn't always going to be easy. But that's what I'd have to face in my **battle for good against evil.**

As long as I shared that mission with Joe and Bec, it was a mission I was prepared to face.

The End

About the Author

When Karen Tayleur was growing up, her father told her many stories about his own childhood. These stories continued to grow. She says, "I always enjoyed the retelling, and wanted to create a character who had the same abilities with 'bending the truth.'" And David Mortimore Baxter was born! Karen lives in Australia with her husband, two children, two cats, and one dog.

About the Illustrator

Brann Garvey grew up in the great state of Iowa, where he studied art and visual communications. He graduated from the Minneapolis College of Art & Design with a degree in illustration. Brann is usually found with one or more of the following: a pencil in his hand, a comic book, a remote for watching DVDs, or his pet kitty, Iggy. When the weather is nice, Brann likes to play disc golf, and he proudly points out that Iowa is one of the world's centers for the sport. Iggy does not play.

agency (AY-juhn-see)—a business that provides a service to the public

badge (BAJ)—a small sign with a message, name, or picture on it, which is pinned to the clothes

case (KAYSS)—a mystery that is being investigated

detective (di-TEK-tiv)—someone who investigates crimes or mysteries

investigation (in-vess-tug-AY-shuhn)—if you have an investigation, or investigate something, you find out whatever you can about something

pachyderm (PAK-uh-durm)—a very large mammal with thick skin, such as an elephant or hippopotamus

sabotage (SAB-uh-tahzh)—damage of property

spy (SPYE)—someone who secretly collects information about someone else

suspect (SUHSS-pekt)—someone thought to be responsible for a crime

win-win (WIN-WIN)—if a situation is win-win, it will be good for everyone involved

1. Why did Victor want to win the trip to Disneyland?

2. Has your school ever had a talent show? If you were going to be in a talent show, what would you do? Talk about the different talents that people can show off for others.

3. What is the difference between spying and solving mysteries? Do you think that the Secret Club was doing the right thing by trying to solve the mysteries in this book? What would you have done? Talk about it.

1. In this book, David's class decides to raise money for Victor's sister, who's sick. If you were asked to raise money and give it to someone else or to a group, who would you give it to? Why? Write about it.

2. Create your own detective agency. What is your agency's name? What kind of mysteries will you solve? Who will be your clients? Don't forget to draw a picture of what your badge will look like.

3. In this book, Tom and Jake collect Sagankiti cards. What do you collect? Write about your collection and why you choose to collect it.

MORE FUN

David Mortimore Baxter

David is a great kid, but he has one big problem — he can't stop talking. These wildly humorous stories, told by David himself, will show readers just how much trouble a boy and his mouth can get into, whether he's going on a class trip, trying to find a missing neighbor, running a detective agency, or getting lost in the wild. David is amiable, engaging, cool, and smart enough to realize that growing up is the biggest adventure of all.